DREAMWORKS
DRAGONS

How to
PICK YOUR
DRAGON

adapted by Erica David

Ready-to-Read

Simon Spotlight
New York   London   Toronto   Sydney   New Delhi

SIMON SPOTLIGHT
An imprint of Simon & Schuster Children's Publishing Division
1230 Avenue of the Americas, New York, New York 10020
First Simon Spotlight edition January 2015
DreamWorks Dragons: Riders of Berk © 2015 DreamWorks Animation LLC. All Rights Reserved.
All rights reserved, including the right of reproduction in whole or in part in any form.
SIMON SPOTLIGHT, READY-TO-READ, and colophon are registered trademarks of Simon & Schuster, Inc.
For information about special discounts for bulk purchases, please contact Simon & Schuster Special Sales at
1-866-506-1949 or business@simonandschuster.com.
Manufactured in the United States of America 1214 LAK
2 4 6 8 10 9 7 5 3 1
ISBN 978-1-4814-2806-4 (hc)
ISBN 978-1-4814-2805-7 (pbk)
ISBN 978-1-4814-2807-1 (eBook)

Chief Stoick was a proud leader.
He did everything the Viking way.
But sometimes the Viking way
was the hard way.

His son, Hiccup, knew another way.
It was the dragon way.
Dragons could help make life easier.
Hiccup convinced Stoick to learn
how to fly a dragon.

Hiccup and his dragon, Toothless,
offered to teach Stoick to ride.
Stoick was eager to learn.
"Whoa, Dad," Hiccup said.
"Before you ride, you have to show
the dragon he can trust you."

Hiccup placed Stoick's hand
on Toothless' snout.
Toothless closed his eyes
and lowered his head.
It was a sign of trust.

Stoick was eager for
the next lesson.
He jumped onto Toothless' back
and took off into the sky.

Hiccup warned Stoick to go slowly.
But he didn't listen.
Hiccup frowned.
His dad had a lot to learn.

The next morning,
Hiccup couldn't find Toothless.
He looked all over for him.
At last, Stoick appeared.
Stoick was riding Toothless.

Stoick was excited.
"We've been all over the village,"
Stoick said. "With Toothless,
being chief has never been so easy!"

"But, Dad," Hiccup said,
"Toothless is my dragon.
You can't just take him."
Stoick looked thoughtful.
"All right, so find me a dragon
of my own," Stoick replied.

Hiccup took Stoick to the
Dragon Training Academy.
Hiccup's friends were eager
to help the chief pick a dragon.

Snotlout brought out Hookfang.
"He is a Monstrous Nightmare,
the only dragon strong enough for
big men like us," he told the chief.

Next, Astrid showed off
her dragon, Stormfly.
"Just because she is beautiful,
it doesn't mean she's not tough,"
Astrid said.

Finally, Fishlegs introduced
his dragon, Meatlug.
"How could you not love
a Gronckle?" he asked Stoick.

Stoick liked all the dragons.
But he couldn't find one he liked
as much as Toothless.

Suddenly, a message arrived
for Chief Stoick.
It said that one of his fishing boats
was in trouble!
Stoick and Hiccup hopped onto
Toothless' back and flew
to the rescue!

The fishing boat was under attack
by a Thunderdrum dragon.

He was stealing the Vikings' fish!

Stoick fought the Thunderdrum
and captured him.
He was very impressed by
the dragon's strength.
"This is the one, Hiccup!
I've found my dragon!" Stoick said.

Stoick brought the Thunderdrum back
to the Dragon Training Academy.
Then he asked Hiccup
to help train his new dragon.

"Be gentle, Dad. Remember,
he has to trust you," Hiccup said.
But Stoick didn't listen.
He and the Thunderdrum
fought and fought . . .

. . . until the Thunderdrum escaped!
Stoick and Hiccup tracked
the dragon to a cave far away.
Another dragon was there, too.

There, they discovered that the Thunderdrum had a secret. The dragon's friend was hurt! "He's trying to help his friend!" Stoick said. "That's why he took our fish!"

Stoick sent Hiccup to get help
for the wounded dragon.
As soon as Hiccup left, a pack of
wild boars charged the cave!
It was up to Stoick and the
Thunderdrum to fight them.

Stoick gently placed his hand on the Thunderdrum's snout. "I want to help. Trust me," he told the dragon.

The Thunderdrum closed his eyes
and lowered his head.
Again, it was a sign of trust.

Stoick took off the dragon's muzzle,
then climbed onto its back.

They fought the wild boars
as a team! And they won!

Later, Hiccup returned with
help for the wounded dragon.
By that time, Stoick and the
Thunderdrum were old friends.
"Look at us, we're bonded,"
Stoick said.

Hiccup smiled.
His dad had just learned
an important lesson.

The Viking way could also be
the dragon way.